A Horse for Hannah

TREASURED HORSES COLLECTION™

titles in Large-Print Editions:

Changing Times

Christmas in Silver Lake

Colorado Summer

The Flying Angels

A Horse for Hannah

Kate's Secret Plan

Louisiana Blue

Pretty Lady of Saratoga

Pride of the Green Mountains

Ride of Courage

Riding School Rivals

Rush for Gold

Spirit of the West

The Stallion of Box Canyon

A HORSE FOR HANNAH

The story of a Boston girl and her journey to England,
where she meets her dream horse, a gentle Hackney

Written by **Coleen Hubbard**
Illustrated by **Sandy Rabinowitz**
Cover Illustration by **Christa Keiffer**
Developed by Nancy Hall, Inc.

Gareth Stevens Publishing
MILWAUKEE

For a free color catalog describing Gareth Stevens' list of high-quality books and
multimedia programs, call 1-800-542-2595 (USA) or 1-800-461-9120 (Canada).
Gareth Stevens Publishing's Fax: (414) 225-0377.

Library of Congress Cataloging-in-Publication Data

A horse for Hannah / written by Coleen Hubbard;
illustrated by Sandy Rabinowitz; cover illustration by Christa Keiffer.
p. cm.
Originally published: Dyersville, Iowa: Ertl Co., 1998.
(Treasured horses collection)
Summary: Although at first unhappy that her birthday present is a trip to
England and not a horse, Hannah falls in love with an English Hackney
and is distressed that she may have to leave the gentle horse behind.
ISBN 0-8368-2402-4 (lib. bdg.)
[1. Horses—Fiction. 2. England—Fiction.] I. Rabinowitz, Sandy, ill.
II. Title. III. Series: Treasured horses collection.
PZ7.H85668Ho   1999
[Fic]—dc21   99-12115

This edition first published in 1999 by
Gareth Stevens Publishing
1555 North RiverCenter Drive, Suite 201
Milwaukee, Wisconsin 53212 USA

© 1998 by Nancy Hall, Inc.
First published by The ERTL Company, Inc., Dyersville, Iowa.

Treasured Horses Collection is a registered trademark of The ERTL Company, Inc.

Printed in the United States of America

1 2 3 4 5 6 7 8 9 03 02 01 00 99

CONTENTS

CHAPTER ONE

Hannah's Birthday

Hannah Brooks studied the two dresses that Fiona, her nanny, had spread across the canopied bed. One was blue silk and the other, a pale lavender.

"Which should I wear, Fiona?" Hannah asked. "Which one would look best for my birthday dinner with Father?"

Fiona put her arm around Hannah's shoulders and squeezed her tight. "Ah, I can't believe you'll be turnin' eleven! While my back was turned you've been transformed into a grown-up lass!"

Hannah laughed at the vivacious young Irish woman who had been her nanny and constant companion for the past five years. "Fiona, you still think I'm six years old! You still think you can sing me to sleep and bribe me with cinnamon pudding."

"The truth is I do still sing you to sleep, and you do still love my puddin'," Fiona teased. "And we both know it!"

Hannah laughed. It was true. Fiona faithfully sat in the rocking chair near her bed every night and sang sweet Irish lullabies as Hannah drifted off to sleep. Hannah's mother had died when she was a baby, and Fiona filled the empty spot in the girl's heart, serving as mother, and friend.

"I think you should wear the blue dress," Fiona said. She ran her hands across the soft, expensive fabric. "It's more suitin' for a fancy birthday dinner with the handsome Captain Brooks, don't you know."

"I wish you were coming with us to the hotel," said Hannah, pulling the dress over her petticoats and smoothing the pleats.

"Now, Hannah, wouldn't that be a sight for all of Boston to see! Your father, the sea captain, takin' his daughter's nanny out on the town. The folks around Beacon Hill would be cluckin' their tongues about that, now wouldn't they! And my fiancé, Jack, wouldn't like it so much either."

"Sometimes being part of Beacon Hill society is such a bother," Hannah said with a sigh. "There are so many things you're not supposed to do."

Fiona began brushing Hannah's long auburn hair. "Listen to you! The daughter of a wealthy sea captain who lives in one of Boston's finest neighborhoods and has a very excitin' life talkin' about the bother of it all!"

Hannah pinned up her hair while Fiona tied the sash of the dress and hooked a ruby necklace around Hannah's neck. Hannah looked in the mirror and studied the glimmering red rubies, a gift from her father for her eighth birthday. He bought them on a voyage to South America—a voyage that Hannah herself had shared.

"You're right, Fiona," Hannah admitted. "I do have an exciting life. Not every girl gets to sail around the world with her father on his own ship, or live in a grand house."

"Or go to the very best schools," Fiona added.

"Yes," said Hannah softly. "Believe me, I'm grateful. And I'm so lucky to have you! But sometimes, just sometimes, I wish—"

"What do you wish, my darlin'?"

"I wish I had a mother, of course. And a father who worked in Boston and didn't have to be away all the time. And—" She looked shyly up at Fiona. "Sisters. I've always wanted sisters. I'm so lonely sometimes. I can hardly bear it."

"Ah, sisters can be a comfort," said Fiona, plucking Hannah's bonnet from the wardrobe. "As you well know, I have six back home in Ireland."

"How much fun it must have been to have such a big family," said Hannah.

"Fun and noisy!" Fiona said with a laugh. "I do miss them. I keep hopin' one of them will be brave and come over to America."

"We're lucky to have each other," said Hannah, hugging Fiona.

"That we are, Miss Hannah Brooks. And now, I have a small gift to present to you for your birthday."

Fiona left the room for a moment and returned with a small package wrapped in white paper and tied with a red bow. Hannah recognized the box immediately. "Chocolates! From Bartels! My favorites!

Oh, Fiona, it's the perfect gift!"

"But," Fiona said, wagging her finger, "not a one until after dinner. I can't have you spoilin' your appetite on your birthday."

"I know!" said Hannah. "When I get home tonight, we'll each have a piece. I know you like the caramels and the cherry cordials."

"If you insist," said Fiona. "It would be rude to refuse you on your birthday."

"Speaking of birthday gifts, do you think Father is going to give me my own horse? It's the only thing I've asked for, and you know he almost always says yes."

"Your father doesn't have the heart to refuse you anything. I'm not sayin' it's the best thing to give a child everything she asks for, but I do understand it. That poor man feels bad being away so much, especially as you don't even have a mother to make his leaving a bit more bearable."

Hannah sat on the bed while Fiona bent down to hook the buttons on her polished black boots. Hannah noticed how Fiona's curly red hair escaped its braid and fell against her black dress.

"Maybe I am the tiniest bit spoiled," said Hannah. "But having a horse would be so lovely, Fiona. Something all my own!"

Fiona finished with the boots and gave Hannah's dress one last tug. "Your sudden love of horses wouldn't have anything to do with your schoolmate who lives out in the country, now would it?" she asked.

"It's true," Hannah agreed. "When I went to Sarah's house last month and rode with her, we had a wonderful time."

"But you were also a bit frightened, you told me. Weren't you?"

"Only because I thought I might fall off. But I didn't. Besides, if I had my own horse, I would take riding lessons and become very good at it."

Just then a bell sounded from downstairs. Fiona straightened Hannah's bonnet. "Your carriage is here. It's time to go meet your father."

"I still wish you were coming along," said Hannah, as she descended the stairs to the front entry with its black and white marble floor.

As the driver held open the door to the carriage, Hannah lifted her skirts and slid inside. She was off to meet her father and, fingers crossed, perhaps her new horse as well!

CHAPTER
TWO

Father's Surprise

As the driver guided his horse to the curb outside the Ritz Hotel, Hannah spotted her father waiting for her. He tipped his tall black hat as she stepped out of the carriage.

"Happy Birthday, Hannah!" he boomed in his rich, deep voice.

Hannah hugged her father, noticing that he had changed out of his captain's uniform and into a well-tailored suit. His white hair and beard framed his distinctive face, which was tanned and weathered from a life at sea.

"When did you get back?" she asked him. "And how was your trip?"

"We docked this afternoon, and the trip to California proved uneventful."

"That was good timing to make it back exactly on my birthday," said Hannah. "Just like you promised."

"Only a shipwreck would have prevented me from missing your birthday. And even then I would have swum across the ocean to be with you."

Hannah laughed at her father's exaggerated style. He was known for his charming way of speaking and wonderful storytelling. "I've missed you, Father. You've been away so much this year."

Captain Brooks guided his daughter inside the hotel to the elegant restaurant. They were seated at the best table, which overlooked the park and was set with fine linens and china.

"The year has been a busy one," said Captain Brooks. "And I've missed you dearly. Happily, I have the good fortune to be home for three weeks now." He picked up the leather-bound menu. "And I have a very special surprise to tell you about."

Hannah tingled with anticipation. A horse! He just had to mean a horse! She tried to sit still and remain calm while her father ordered oysters on the half shell, baked fish, peas and potatoes, and a frozen pudding for dessert. She thought he would never finish discussing the selections with the waiter.

Finally, the waiter scurried to the kitchen, and Captain Brooks turned and smiled at Hannah. "Can you guess what I've arranged for your eleventh birthday? Do you have any idea?"

"I think so," said Hannah, trying to hide her grin behind a napkin. "Does it have four legs and a tail and eat grain for its supper?"

Captain Brooks looked surprised and sat up straighter in his chair. "What are you talking about?" he asked.

"Don't tease me, Father," Hannah said. "You know, a horse. The only thing I want in the whole world is a horse of my own."

"Oh, a horse! Now I understand—four legs, a tail! I was confused for a minute."

"What kind did you get, Father? What color? Where is it?"

Captain Brooks was silent, stroking his beard with his hand.

"Father, what is it?"

"Hannah, I don't know what to say. I feel terrible, but I didn't get you a horse. We talked about this before I left."

Hannah felt tears of disappointment stinging her eyes. But she knew a lady must mind her manners. She sat still, her hands in her lap, as she had been taught to do as a small child.

"Hannah, darling. We live in the middle of a big city. We don't need a horse. If we need a carriage, we can step out on the street and hire one. If you want to ride, we can rent a horse at a livery."

"That's true," said Hannah quietly. "But it's not the same as having one of your own."

"Perhaps. But, Hannah, wait until you hear what my gift is. I hope it will more than make up for the lack of a horse. Shall I tell you now?"

Hannah nodded, not trusting herself to speak. She felt as though she had swallowed a rock.

"Hannah, in three weeks' time, when I set sail for London, you shall accompany me."

"Truly?" Hannah was surprised. For the past three years, she hadn't been allowed to sail with her father. He had insisted it was time for her to stay in Boston and concentrate on her studies.

"I have business in London for a couple of weeks. And while I'm there, you are going to stay with my cousin and his family on their farm."

"You mean Uncle Ethan and Aunt Jane?"

"And their two daughters, Polly and Mary. They're just about your age, and it's time you meet your English relatives and see the part of the world where I was born."

Hannah didn't know what to say. Her birthday wasn't turning out at all as she'd expected. Not only wasn't she getting a horse, she was also being made to stay with relatives she didn't know.

"They're very excited to meet you, Hannah," her father said. "And imagine what business Ethan is in. He raises horses—a breed called Hackney. You'll be around horses all day long!"

"Truly?" asked Hannah, brightening. "Will I be allowed to ride?"

"I'm sure you will. Ethan has warned me, however, that Polly and Mary have certain responsibilities with the horses. It's possible you'll be asked to help out."

"I would love that!" said Hannah.

She took a forkful of potatoes and imagined herself brushing the horses until their silky coats shined, and leading them to pasture to munch on sweet grass. She imagined herself riding through the rolling green countryside with her cousins, who were undoubtedly fashionable and proper and very British.

She couldn't wait to tell Fiona. Perhaps a trip away from Boston was just what she needed. And maybe her cousins, Polly and Mary, would provide the experience she longed for of having sisters.

"Thank you, Father," said Hannah as the frozen

berry pudding arrived at the table, complete with two pink sugar roses. "It's a wonderful birthday."

Captain Brooks took his daughter's hand and held it between his own rough hands. "I've missed your smile," he said. "*Cloud Song* will sing once again with you on board."

Cloud Song *Sets Sail*

66 "Welcome aboard!" boomed Captain Brooks, offering his daughter a hand as she stepped onto the main deck of *Cloud Song*.

"It's wonderful to be aboard!" Hannah replied. She looked around the ship with affection. "I can't wait to set sail."

Cloud Song was one of dozens of clipper ships docked in Boston Harbor. The elegant wooden ships with their huge canvas sails were sometimes called "tea clippers" because their cargo often included tea and because they were so fast they simply "clipped off the miles."

The deck bustled with activity as sailors climbed

the rigging to unfurl the enormous sails. Other sailors were cleaning the wooden decks, stowing gear, and loading cargo down below. The men called to each other in several languages as they performed their difficult work, weaving around the three tall masts and miles of rope.

"Well, make yourself at home in the after cabin," said Captain Brooks. "As you can see, I have much work to do. But I'll expect you to join me on the poop deck once we're under sail."

Hannah gave her father a half-serious salute and went below. Her trunk had already been delivered to the captain's quarters, which were as beautifully decorated as their home on Beacon Hill. All around there were small, square windows to let in light, with heavy shutters in case of bad weather.

The quarters consisted of several staterooms for sleeping, a bathroom, and a parlor known as the main saloon. Meals were taken in the forward cabin, which held a dining room, pantry, kitchen, and more staterooms for the ship's steward and mates.

Though the furniture was bolted down, the rooms were filled with luxurious carpets, paintings, and carved wooden cabinets trimmed with gold leaf. Once the ship was under sail, Hannah knew the steward would set out the china tea sets, framed photographs, music boxes, and statues, making the cabin look even more like home.

Hannah was too excited to unpack. She wanted to hurry back to the deck and share in the anticipation of readying *Cloud Song* for her twelve-day journey to England. But just as she stepped outside the door, Hannah almost ran directly into the ship's cook, a gray–haired gentleman named Duncan.

"Hello, Miss Hannah," he said, smiling. "I heard you will be sailing with us once again."

"Hello, Duncan," Hannah said. "How nice to see you."

"It's been too long, Miss Hannah, since we've had you aboard."

"I know, Duncan. Father has wanted me to stay in Boston to go to school these last three years. I've missed the sea!"

"The Captain is right. School is important, and the sea will always be here. I just wanted to let you know that I've collected some of your favorite foods for the journey. Oranges, raisins, salmon, and even a bit of chocolate. You still are fond of chocolate?"

"Always!" Hannah replied with a laugh. "Thank you, Duncan."

"See you at dinner, Miss Hannah."

Duncan disappeared down the narrow hallway,

and Hannah climbed the short stairway to the deck. She passed sailors as they performed their difficult and dangerous work. They climbed nimbly up rope ladders, called ratlines, and out onto the long poles, called yards, attached to the masts. It sometimes took her breath away to imagine climbing so high, with only a single footrope to keep one from plunging into the sea.

Hannah wasn't allowed to talk to the men while they were working, so she found an out-of-the-way corner. Being the daughter of a sea captain, she knew that *Cloud Song* had thirty-three sails, made from over two acres of canvas. She also knew the names of the various kinds of sails—the topsails, jibs, topgallantsails, royals, and studdingsails.

From the time she was old enough to walk about the ship, Captain Brooks had made a point of teaching Hannah about the sea, the winds, and navigation. He loved to tell her the wondrous story of how she had been born at sea, during a storm, on a long voyage to China.

"How many girls can claim such a beginning?" he always said to Hannah. "My daughter—Princess of the Seas!"

Hours later, when *Cloud Song* was fully under sail, Hannah joined her father on the poop deck. This was a small, open deck at the rear of the ship where the captain kept watch of the sea and his men.

"May I keep you company?" Hannah asked.

"Certainly!" Captain Brooks replied. "She's a well–found ship, isn't she?"

"She is!" Hannah agreed. "I'm so happy to be sailing with you, Father."

"So you approve of my birthday gift, Princess of the Seas?"

"How could I not?" said Hannah. "I get to sail. I get to see a new country. I get to meet my cousins. And best of all, I get to be around horses!"

"Still dreaming of horses?"

"It's true, Father. I do think about them quite a lot. I know I can't have one of my own, but you have to admit—they *are* beautiful and mysterious."

Captain Brooks laughed and hugged his daughter. "For my taste," he said, "I find the sea beautiful and mysterious."

Hannah had to agree. She looked out at the Atlantic Ocean, which was a blue–black color, frosted with white foam. The sky, a lighter shade of blue, formed a distinct line on the horizon where it met the sea. All around them the vast waters rolled and rocked and splashed over the decks of *Cloud Song*. The wind sent sea spray into their faces, bringing the smell of salt and fish—and mystery.

"It *is* beautiful!" Hannah cried, turning her face into the wind.

"Well, don't just stand there, Hannah. Get to work."

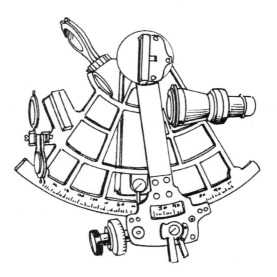

Captain Brooks opened a wooden box and took out two instruments used to plan a ship's journey. One, a sextant, measured the altitude of the sun, moon, stars, and planets. The other, a chronometer, measured time.

"You can do some calculations while I write in my logbook," he told her.

"I hope I remember how," Hannah said, taking the

instruments. "It's been a long time."

"True," said her father. "But all the mathematics you've been studying at school will certainly help. And don't forget, your mother was one of the most gifted navigators I ever met."

"I wish I could remember her. I wish she was with us right now."

"I do too," answered Captain Brooks, his voice lowering to a whisper. "But I must tell you, Hannah, I do believe she is with us. She is with us in all this beauty. And she is with us when I look at your face and see her eyes."

Hannah smiled and turned the sextant over in her hands. My mother was a navigator, she thought. Then, turning her thoughts to the angle of the sun and the seconds ticking away on the chronometer, she smoothed the weathered map before her and began to work.

Later, after a formal dinner of salmon, potatoes, and green beans, Hannah went back up on deck once again. The sky was completely dark now, and thousands of brilliant stars blazed above her. Hannah pulled her woolen shawl tighter around her shoulders and looked up to spot the constellations. She located the Big Dipper and Orion and spotted several especially bright stars that were most likely planets.

Night was Hannah's favorite time of all on *Cloud Song*. She loved the sound of the great ship slipping through the dark water. She loved the stars and the fresh air and the calmness.

As time passed, many of the sailors who weren't on watch gathered on deck to sing. One young sailor played an accordion; another joined in on an ancient fiddle. As everyone sang together, Hannah closed her eyes and listened to the familiar songs. Some were mournful tunes about life on the sea, but many had funny, complicated rhymes that made everyone laugh. Hannah felt a sense of belonging—to *Cloud Song* and to generations of people who sailed the world looking for treasure and adventure.

The ship rocked gently, and Hannah felt her eyelids grow heavy. It would feel good to sleep, she thought. Sleeping on a ship was a special pleasure, at least to those who weren't seasick. Hannah always had vivid dreams when she sailed.

Tonight, she thought, I'll try to dream about riding with Polly and Mary across the English countryside.

Meeting the Cousins

After twelve days on *Cloud Song*, Hannah could barely walk on solid ground. As she took her first steps off the ship, her legs wobbled beneath her, and her head felt light.

"Steady," said Captain Brooks, taking her by the elbow. "Take it slowly. Keep breathing."

Soon Hannah felt better. She walked slowly toward the street with her father, amazed by the sights and sounds and smells of London. "We're finally here!" she said. "We're in England!"

"I'll get a carriage," said her father, holding out his hand. The streets were crowded with hundreds of horses pulling carriages, carts, and hansom cabs.

How did all of the people and animals manage to get where they needed to go without constantly running into each other? Why London was much more crowded than Boston!

A hansom cab, pulled by two large black horses, stopped at the side of the brick-paved street. The driver tipped his hat and said, "Where to, mates?" His accent was so strange to Hannah's ears that she barely understood him.

"We would like to have a proper English meal," said Captain Brooks. "What do you recommend?"

"I know just the place," replied the driver.

As they made their way through the bustling streets, Captain Brooks pointed out the sights. They saw the famous clock called Big Ben, and then The Houses of Parliament where members of government met to enact laws.

"What's that?" gasped Hannah, staring at a huge iron and glass structure.

"That," explained her father, "is called the Crystal Palace. It is being built to house 19,000 exhibits for The Great Exhibition."

"How beautiful!" Hannah exclaimed. "London is so grand. I wish we could stay and see everything!"

But after eating a dinner of liver, bacon, potatoes, and gooseberry pie in a traditional chop house,

Captain Brooks hurried them back outside to the street to hire a covered carriage.

"We have a long drive to Shady Glenn and then I must return immediately to London."

The two settled into the soft leather seats while the driver attached Hannah's large trunk to the top of the carriage.

"I hope I brought the right clothes," said Hannah. "London seems quite sophisticated."

"I think you'll find the fashions a bit less fussy out in the country," said Captain Brooks. "Even though Ethan is a gentleman farmer with many acres of land, the style of life will be different than you are accustomed to."

Hannah sensed that her father was trying to warn her about something, but she wasn't quite sure what he meant. She closed her eyes, tired from her journey, and tried to picture her cousins Mary and Polly. In her mind they had auburn hair, just like her own, and wore matching velvet dresses of deep, deep blue. All three of them laughed in the wind as they rode their English horses.

Sometime much later, as Hannah was fast asleep, the carriage hit a hole in the road. It pitched to the left, throwing Hannah against her father.

"What is it?" Hannah asked, alarmed and

wide awake. "Where are we?"

"Nothing to be alarmed over. The left wheel caught a hole, that's all," explained Captain Brooks. "Everything's fine. We're almost there."

"We are?" asked Hannah, straightening up. "I slept all the way?"

"Afraid so," her father said. "At least you'll be well rested when it's time to meet our relatives."

Hannah gazed outside the carriage window at the open countryside, green and damp and quite beautiful. The hills sloped gently on both sides of the road, with tall hedges marking the boundaries between properties. Their carriage passed several enormous houses with mile-long driveways.

"The houses here look so fancy!" exclaimed Hannah. "Will Uncle Ethan's house look like that?"

"Not quite so large, I imagine. I've never seen it. I went to Boston with my family when Uncle Ethan and I were small boys, remember. We've exchanged letters and pictures, but I've never seen his farm or his family."

Soon the driver slowed his horses to a trot and turned the carriage up a narrow lane that veered off the main road. The trees were thick, so it took a few moments before the farm came into view. The horses stopped, and Hannah and her father were silent.

"You've arrived," said the driver, coming around to open the door of the carriage. "This is Shady Glenn."

Hannah stepped out, holding up her dress so as not to drag it in a deep puddle of muddy water. Before her stood an ancient two-story house made of crumbling stone. Hannah couldn't believe her eyes. In all her dreams, she had never imagined Shady Glenn to be so dilapidated, so run down. Where was the grand English home she had pictured a thousand times? This house had a chimney that sagged, stone walls blackened by smoke, and window shutters broken and hanging. Hannah gulped and reached for her father's hand.

"It certainly has a lived-in feeling to it," said Captain Brooks brightly, squeezing Hannah's hand.

Before Hannah could answer, the front door opened. Ethan and Jane Brooks emerged from the house and hustled over to greet them. Ethan was tall and sober looking, while Jane was short and plump and all smiles and dimples. Her blonde hair was held back by a red kerchief, and she wore a stained apron over a gray dress that had seen better days.

"Welcome!" Jane called out, waving excitedly. "Welcome, welcome! We've been waiting for you!" Her voice, warm and sweet, lacked the clipped, formal

tone of the people Hannah had heard in London.

Jane ran to hug Hannah, not seeming to mind a bit as she stepped into a muddy puddle. She laughed and pulled Hannah to her, exclaiming over her height.

"You're so tall, like Ethan," she said. "Polly and Mary are short, just like me."

"Where are Polly and Mary?" Hannah asked.

"With the horses," replied Ethan. "Go round and find them and bring them back for tea. Will you stay for tea, Samuel?" He stood awkwardly, his hands in his pockets, smiling at his cousin, the rich sea captain from America.

"Of course!" said Captain Brooks. "I'll have to leave tonight, but we'll have several days together when I return for Hannah. Go on, Hannah, and find your cousins. You've been waiting for this moment for weeks and weeks."

Hannah studied her father's face and realized he wanted her to go and meet her cousins without making a fuss. She had been raised to be polite and gracious at all times, so she took a deep breath and stepped gingerly through the puddles.

Behind the house were several stables and outbuildings, all built of weathered gray wood. The roof of the closest stable looked as though it might collapse at any moment. All over the grounds were empty barrels, broken farm equipment, and mud and more mud.

Hannah peered inside the first stable. It was dark and musty, but clean. It was also empty. Hannah wondered where the horses were, but then figured they must be out to pasture. She walked to the second stable and spotted a man in knickers and boots pushing a wheelbarrow of straw.

"Hello," said Hannah, "I'm Hannah Brooks, Mary and Polly's cousin. Could you please tell me where they can be found?"

"Inside," said the man, pointing. His front teeth were missing, but he smiled anyway. "I'm Derek. You're the relative from America, eh? We don't get many from America in these parts. Careful of the mud. It's the muddy season."

"I've noticed," said Hannah with a smile. "Pleased to meet you, Derek."

"Pleased to meet you, Miss. Go on in. Best be careful of the younger one, Polly. She bites." At this, Derek laughed and laughed, slapping his knee and wiping his eyes.

Not knowing what to think, Hannah stepped inside the stable. A strong acrid odor assailed her, and she took out a handkerchief to cover her nose before proceeding further. It took awhile for her eyes to adjust to the darkness of the stalls. When they did, she saw her cousins, hard at work in one of the back stalls. They were both blonde like Aunt Jane, and dressed much the same. They wore kerchiefs and aprons and tall black boots. They were shoveling what looked to be more mud into a wheelbarrow.

"Hello!" called Hannah, trying to make her voice friendly.

Both girls turned around and stared at Hannah, not speaking. But then the taller of the two walked over and held out her hand.

"Are you Hannah?" she asked. When she smiled she looked like Aunt Jane.

Hannah put away her handkerchief and shook her hand. "I am. And you must be Mary."

"Yes, that's right," said Mary. "This is my sister, Polly. She's eleven. I'm thirteen."

"Hello, Polly," said Mary.

Polly said nothing. She stared at Hannah and at her American cousin's expensive dress and bonnet with hard, unsmiling eyes.

"You won't be wanting those kind of dresses here," Polly finally muttered. "Not to muck out stables."

"What do you mean?" asked Hannah.

"Back in Boston you have servants to do all your

work," snapped Polly. "But here, everyone helps with the horses. And that includes you. So you had better get used to getting your pretty silk dresses all messed up."

Hannah was stunned, not knowing how she should respond to this attack. Why was Polly acting so hostile to her when they had only just met? What could she have done or said to offend her?

Mary, twisting her apron and looking worried, said nothing.

They don't want me here! thought Hannah. Why did I ever come?

Hannah tried to think of something to say. "Is that—is that horse manure you're shoveling?" She tried to sound interested, but she couldn't think of anything more disgusting and smelly! She wanted to *ride* horses, not clean up after them. Her father had never said a word about wearing boots and walking around in *horse manure*!

Polly and Mary laughed at her squeamishness, and Polly began marching around the stable with her nose in the air, repeating in a snooty voice, "Is that horse manure you're shoveling?"

"Stop it, Polly," Mary finally said. "That's enough."

But Polly didn't stop pretending to be Hannah. She continued to tiptoe around the stable, holding her nose.

Hannah looked at Polly and tried to keep her voice even. "I may not know much about horses," she said, "but at least I know my manners."

Then Hannah turned and ran out of the stable. She passed Derek, but she didn't stop until she reached the front door of the house. Inside, she found her father in front of the fire with Ethan and Jane, sipping tea from cracked cups and eating brown bread with butter.

"May I speak with you, Father?" she asked.

Captain Brooks responded to the urgency in his daughter's voice, and asked to be excused. He followed Hannah outside and closed the door.

"Oh, Father!" she cried, as soon as she was sure they were alone, "Please don't leave me here! Please don't make me stay in this horrible place! My cousins hate me. They're out in the barn mocking me as we speak!"

Hannah hugged her father tightly, as tears streamed down her face.

"It's not for long," her father soothed. "Only two weeks and then I'll be back for you. You can get along till then, can't you? You're just having a bad start. You'll make friends with your cousins. And by the time I get back, you'll be an expert horsewoman!"

Hannah said nothing, for she realized that there

was nothing that could be done. Her father had business to attend to in London and wouldn't be able to take care of her at the same time. She had no choice but to make the best of things till he returned.

As she dried her eyes on the handkerchief that her father handed her, she wished with all her heart that she was back in Boston. Her birthday present to visit England and see her cousins was nothing short of a disaster.

Meeting Gwenny

Hannah awoke the next morning not sure
where she was sleeping. It took her a full minute to
realize that she was in the drafty guest bedroom of
her English relatives, covered by a tattered green quilt.
She missed her father and Fiona. And she dreaded
having to face her cousins again, especially Polly.

In the kitchen Aunt Jane and the house servant
named Nora were busy kneading bread dough on an
old wooden board. Aunt Jane smiled at Hannah and
waved a flour-coated hand. Hannah could scarcely
believe that Aunt Jane and Uncle Ethan only had one
house servant and two men to work the farm. At
home she had Fiona in addition to the housekeeper,

the gardener, and the cook.

"Sit down, child. I'll bring you some breakfast. How did you sleep?" Aunt Jane inquired.

"Fine," answered Hannah. "It's very quiet in the countryside. In Boston you hear street sounds all night long."

"It must be so exciting to live in a big city. You'll have to tell me everything about it while you're here with us."

"Where are Polly and Mary?" Hannah asked.

"With Ethan and the horses. They like to finish their work early so they can go riding. Your father tells us you like horses."

"Yes!" exclaimed Hannah. "But I haven't much experience with them. I've only ridden once, and I've never—well, cleaned up after them."

Aunt Jane laughed heartily and brought Hannah a bowl of oatmeal and some bread and butter. "You'll soon catch on," she told Hannah. "And I know the girls will help you. They're thrilled that you're here."

Sure they are, thought Hannah sadly. About as thrilled as having a stomachache. She ate her breakfast, dreading the moment when she had to leave the warm kitchen and her friendly aunt to join her cousins.

"I've left you a pair of tall boots by the back door,"

said Aunt Jane. "I don't think you'll be wanting to ruin those lovely ones you're wearing. And a kerchief will suit you better than a bonnet. In the country we only wear bonnets on market day."

Hannah excused herself and, after thanking Aunt Jane for the food, went back to her bedroom to change her boots. There she noticed something strange. Her trunk was wide open, and Hannah was almost positive that she had closed it before coming downstairs. "Maybe I'm just being forgetful," she told herself.

But when Hannah found her cousins out in the stables, she saw that Polly was wearing her red hair ribbon—the one edged in gold! Hannah couldn't believe that Polly would do such a thing, but there was no mistaking the distinctive ribbon. Hannah took a deep breath and tried to clear her head. Polly must have come inside through the front door and gone upstairs while she was having breakfast and rifled through her belongings.

What should I do? Hannah wondered. Should I say something? She thought about what Fiona would do and remembered Fiona's favorite expression "turn the other cheek." Hannah decided she would ignore the incident and try to be charitable toward her cousin.

"Good morning, Mary. Good morning, Polly," Hannah said. She hoped that her kerchief, apron, and tall boots would show them that she was one of them after all.

"Good morning," Mary greeted her. "How are you today?"

Polly said nothing. But she had a fierce, defiant smile on her pretty face as though she was daring Hannah to say anything about the ribbon.

"I'm fine, thank you," Hannah said. "And eager to work. Mary, will you show me what to do?"

"Come with me," Mary said, leading her toward the back of the stable where it was darker. An overpowering smell of animal waste hit Hannah's nose. "Here's a shovel and a wheelbarrow. After you muck out the first stall, you can scrub it out with a mop. Then fill it with fresh straw."

"Oh," said Hannah, trying not to wrinkle her nose. "Where are the horses?"

"Grazing in the pasture. I'll take you there when we've cleaned up. All right, then?"

Hannah was determined not to show her distaste for the hard work. Taking a deep breath, she tried to think of pleasant things while she shoveled and mopped, like learning to ride properly and returning home to Boston.

When she had finished two stalls, Hannah looked down at herself and saw that her dress, apron, and boots were wet and soiled.

I smell like a barn, she thought. And I must look just terrible. My friends at school would never believe this!

After several hours had passed, Mary announced that they could take a break and go watch the horses. She led Hannah out of the stable, and Polly followed, twisting the red hair ribbon and smiling with obvious delight.

In the fenced pasture a dozen horses grazed contentedly. Hannah stared wide-eyed at the beautiful animals. Though their color and markings varied, all of the horses shared a similar build and gait.

"These are all Hackney horses?" Hannah asked.

"Yes," Mary said. "We breed them. They're a truly

English horse, dating back at least a hundred years."

"What makes them so special?" inquired Hannah.

"They're good travel horses," said Mary. "They're fast under the saddle, and they make wonderful carriage horses."

"They're so pretty," Hannah said breathlessly.

"They're so pretty," Polly repeated, mocking her cousin. "Believe me, there is nothing pretty about horses. All they do is eat, make a mess, and eat some more!"

Hannah was shocked by her cousin's outburst. How could Polly not love being surrounded by her family's horses? Even if what she had said about the mess *was* partly true.

"Polly doesn't appreciate farm life the way my parents and I do," Mary explained. "She prefers the finer things in life."

"That's right. And when I'm old enough, I'm moving to the city," Polly proclaimed. "I'll never have to clean out another stall again."

Just then, one of the horses left the group and made its way slowly toward the girls. Hannah turned to watch, struck by the singular beauty of the chestnut-colored horse.

"What's that one's name?" Hannah asked, pointing.

"That's Gwenny," Mary answered. "She's a dear one. Very friendly but very strong."

Hannah watched as the horse came closer. Her coat was brown with red highlights, and her mane and tail were just a half shade lighter. She had a white stripe down her face and white markings above each hoof. Gwenny stopped at the fence and sniffed at the girls, her brown eyes alert and curious.

"May I pet her?" Hannah asked, knowing that she sounded inexperienced.

"Let her sniff your hand first," Mary advised. "And she likes to have her ears stroked."

Mary showed her how, and then Hannah did the same.

Gwenny nickered at Hannah, which made Hannah laugh with pleasure. "Hello, Gwenny," Hannah said. "It's so nice to meet you."

"She's not the queen, you know!" Polly said with a sneer. "You don't have to be so stuffy!"

"She's just being gentle, Polly," Mary said. "Maybe if you were more gentle with the horses, they'd go easier on you." Then Mary explained to Hannah how Polly was always being nipped at by the horses.

I don't doubt it, Hannah thought. If I were a horse, I'd nip at her, too.

"Hannah, would you like to ride Gwenny?"

Mary asked. "She's a smooth ride."

There was nothing in the world that Hannah wanted more than to ride Gwenny. But she was still afraid, and she especially didn't want Polly to find out how inexperienced she was. If Polly knew that the horses seemed large and unpredictable to Hannah, there would be no end to her teasing.

"Maybe tomorrow," Hannah said. "My back is sore from all the shoveling and mopping."

"It will only get worse," Polly said smartly. "If you stay around here very long, you'll have a permanent hump on your back. Your skin will turn gray from all the rain, your hands will be rough as sand, and your hair will look a fright!"

"Really?" asked Hannah in the sweetest voice she could muster. "That's strange because *your* hair looks quite pretty. Especially with that lovely red ribbon."

Polly opened her mouth to speak but then shut it in surprise. Hannah turned and stepped through the mud back to the house. Inside she was fuming. All morning she had endured her cousin's taunts and insults. She had hoped that Polly would give up when she didn't react, but now she understood that no matter what she said or how she acted, Polly was determined not to like her.

The only thing that consoled Hannah was

thinking about Gwenny. If not for Polly, she would have liked to stay and get acquainted with Gwenny. Tomorrow I'll go back and ride her, she decided. If I can sail around the world, I can learn to ride a horse!

Later that night, Hannah sat in front of the fire with her aunt and uncle and cousins. Supper was finished and the dishes put away. Aunt Jane concentrated on a piece of embroidery, while Uncle Ethan read the newspaper. Polly wandered around, unable to sit still. Mary was writing in her diary. Mary said she wanted to write books when she was older, and Hannah could picture her doing just that.

Hannah was glad the day was over and happy for the peaceful quiet of the evening. Her muscles were sore from working. She'd never felt so tired. At home in Boston, she never did housework, much less tended animals or carried in wood for the fire.

Am I truly spoiled? Hannah thought. Do most people work this hard every day? Hannah felt a pang of guilt over her easy life, though she knew it was not of her own choosing. By being born the daughter of Captain Brooks, she enjoyed certain privileges that her cousins did not. On the other hand, they had a mother and she did not.

Hannah watched as Aunt Jane reached over and touched Mary's cheek. The simple gesture made

Hannah's heart skip. What must it feel like to have your mother touch you with such love and affection? Though her cousins had to work hard, at least they could sit happily with their mother at the end of the day.

Suddenly Hannah remembered that she had brought gifts for her relatives. She excused herself and went upstairs. When she returned, she handed wrapped gifts to each of them.

"My favorite pipe tobacco!" exclaimed Uncle Ethan.

"What a beautiful velvet shawl! Thank you, dearie," cried Aunt Jane. "I've never owned anything so special."

Mary was equally thrilled by her scented writing paper and envelopes, though Polly only shrugged over hers.

"And one more thing," Hannah said, bringing out a large white box with a red ribbon. "I don't know if a taste for chocolate runs in the family, but I brought my favorites just in case."

Aunt Jane hugged Hannah and thanked her again. Then she opened the box. "Oh, they're too pretty to eat!"

"No they're not," said Polly, grabbing two at once.

"Mind your manners!" her father scolded. "Cousin

Hannah was thoughtful enough to bring these items all the way across the ocean."

"Thank you," Polly said to Hannah, seeming not to want to anger her parents.

But later, when no one could hear, Polly made sure to get even. She leaned over and whispered to Hannah, "I know you're trying to make good with Mother and Father. But you can't bribe me with a few sweets. You're still a snob from America."

"Maybe I am," Hannah whispered back. "But what is *your* excuse?"

The First Ride

"Do you want to ride Gwenny today?"
Mary asked Hannah.

Several days had passed, and Hannah still hadn't quite worked up enough courage to learn to ride. She kept meaning to, but a little voice inside reminded her that Polly would be nearby to make fun of her if she didn't do things just right. No matter how nice Hannah was to Polly, she was met with a mean-spirited attitude.

At least Mary and Uncle Ethan and Aunt Jane treated her with kindness and tried to make her feel welcome. Still, the visit was hardly as Hannah had imagined. Farm life was hard. Hannah had to keep remembering not to compare everything to the way she was used to living in Boston.

As she brushed Gwenny's shiny chestnut coat, Hannah wished there were a way to ride with just Mary, but Polly never left them alone. But at least, thought Hannah, despite Polly, I have learned to care for Gwenny and the other horses.

Each day Hannah became more used to the cleaning and brushing and feeding. She discovered she loved being around the horses even more than she'd thought possible. She loved watching their movements and trying to read their expressions.

Mary was a good and patient teacher, showing Hannah when a particular horse was tired, hungry, bored, or wanting attention.

"I have an idea," whispered Mary, moving next to Hannah in the stall.

"What?" Hannah whispered back.

"Why don't just you and I take a ride this afternoon?"

"What about Polly?" Hannah asked.

"Don't worry about her. I'll ask Mother to distract her for a few hours."

As Mary walked away, Hannah put her arms around Gwenny's neck. "I'll do my best to ride you today," she whispered. "But you'll have to be a willing partner and show me how."

Gwenny lifted her head and nuzzled Hannah's shoulder. And for that moment, Hannah forgot all about Polly and missing her father and Fiona. She forgot all about the hard work and her cold, drafty room where she now slept. She simply enjoyed the pleasure of Gwenny's warm breath upon her neck.

Later that afternoon, Hannah and Mary met in the stable.

"It's all arranged," said Mary. "Mother has told Polly that she has to stay in the house and help make cheese and butter with her this afternoon."

"Was Polly agreeable?" asked Hannah. She had a feeling she already knew the answer.

"Not entirely. I think she suspects something. But she loves fresh butter, and Mother told her she could eat scones and butter for tea if she helps."

"Thank you," said Hannah. "You're very kind."

"Don't mention it," smiled Mary. "I thought we could ride to the blueberry bushes. I brought a pail for each of us."

Suddenly, the two girls heard the stable door slam.

"What was that?" said Hannah, jumping with surprise.

"I don't know," said Mary. "Probably just Derek."

Hannah hoped that was true, but she had a sinking feeling that Polly had been spying on them.

"Let's get started," said Mary. "The first thing you have to learn is how to work the halter and bridle." She went to the far wall where the tack was hung and returned with her arms full of leather. She patiently instructed Hannah how to fit the halter over Gwenny's head and attach the lead line.

"Like this?" asked Hannah.

"Well done," Mary answered. "Now comes the bridle."

Mary showed how the bridle gave the rider control of the horse and how the reins would become extensions of Hannah's arms. Finally, she showed Hannah how the saddle should be positioned to give comfort to the horse and the rider.

Hannah paid close attention. It was all so confusing. She wondered how long it would take before using the equipment made sense to her.

"I think learning ocean navigation is almost easier than this!" she joked with Mary.

"Oh, how I would love to sail on a ship!" exclaimed Mary. "The thought of that makes riding a horse seem absolutely ordinary!"

"Maybe I'll be able to teach you about sailing sometime. Then I can return the favor of everything you've been teaching me about horses while I'm visiting."

"That would be a dream come true," Mary said.

After Mary saddled her own horse, the two girls led their animals outside. "Are you ready?" Mary asked, putting one foot into the stirrup and swinging her leg over her horse.

For a moment Hannah was too surprised to speak. Mary was riding astride! In Boston, no proper lady would ever ride anything but sidesaddle.

"You're riding astride?" Hannah asked.

"Of course," Mary replied with a laugh. "In the country, it's expected. It's much easier, you know. You try it. Just swing your leg over Gwenny's back."

After a few tries, Hannah was at last seated properly in the saddle. Throughout it all, Gwenny, gentle and cooperative, stood patiently, as if she was used to novice riders.

"Good girl," said Hannah, stroking her neck. "Thank you for waiting."

"Let's go!" cried Mary. She showed Hannah how to nudge the standing horse by using her voice, legs, and the reins.

Hannah imitated Mary, and Gwenny took off, walking slowly behind Mary's horse. "Oh, my!" said Hannah, jerking forward a bit. "I'm actually riding her!"

The First Ride

After just a few minutes of watching Mary, Hannah began to get the feel of riding. She tried to relax into Gwenny's gait and loosen her tight grip on the reins. Eventually she was able to lift her eyes and look around, thrilled by the motion and the lush, green countryside.

"You're doing well," Mary commented, twisting around in the saddle to observe her cousin. "Just don't clench your legs so tightly. Gwenny's a good horse, so you can trust her. She knows what to do."

Too soon they reached a dense clump of bushes, and Mary stopped her horse. "Stay there," she told Hannah, "and I'll help you dismount. That takes a bit of practice. I'll just tie my horse to that tree."

As Hannah turned to watch Mary dismount, a loud and sudden banging noise came from the direction of some nearby bushes. Hannah gasped in surprise as Gwenny startled and abruptly scuttled sideways. Hannah, caught off guard, struggled to keep her balance. For a horrible moment she thought she was going to fall off and be stomped by her gentle new friend.

"Hold on!" shouted Mary, running over to help. Gwenny had quieted down by this time, but she still stood erect, her head held high, as she sniffed the air. She whinnied and snorted, clearly upset. Hannah reached over and stroked her mane.

"Are you all right?" asked Mary, taking the reins and stroking Gwenny's neck.

"I—I think so," gulped Hannah. "I thought I was going to fall."

"I thought so as well," said Mary. "But you did a good job staying on your horse." She helped Hannah dismount.

"What *was* that noise?" Hannah asked.

"I think I know. Stay here," Mary whispered, putting a finger to her lips. She disappeared into the bushes as Hannah watched.

A few seconds later, Mary emerged, dragging Polly behind her. Polly had a sheepish grin on her face and held a tin pail and a brass candlestick.

"Polly?" Hannah asked. "You made the noise?"

"Not intentionally," Polly said. "I just wanted to pick berries."

"With a candlestick?" Mary asked, angrily.

"So that *was* you in the stable this morning," Hannah said.

"Did you think I was going to let you two go off and have all the fun while I slaved over the butter churn?" Polly's eyes flashed defiantly.

"You've been mean and awful to Hannah from the moment she arrived!" Mary scolded. "You're my sister and I love you, but I'm embarrassed by how you've acted. And I'm horrified that you would intentionally scare Hannah's horse. That was dangerous, Polly. Hannah could have been badly hurt!"

Polly's eyes filled with tears. "Are you going to tell Mother and Father?" she asked her sister.

"Yes, I am," Mary answered sternly. "And no doubt you won't be allowed to go to market next week as punishment."

To Hannah's surprise, Polly began to cry. "Please don't tell them," she begged. "I wasn't trying to frighten the horses. I was just playing a joke on you. Market day is the only time I get to leave the farm."

Despite herself, Hannah felt sorry for her cousin. The farm was a rather small and limited world. And she knew that Polly dreamed of a different life.

"We won't tell," Hannah said. "It's all right."

"No, it isn't," Mary said. "Polly knows better. She's been raised around horses. She knows just what a sudden, loud sound can do to animals."

"But I didn't mean to!" Polly cried. "I just wanted to surprise you by being here when you arrived and making a scary noise. I didn't know Hannah was still on her horse."

"Then you must apologize to Hannah. This was her first day riding, and you've ruined it for her."

Polly looked sideways at Hannah, her mouth pulled into a tight frown. She seemed to be weighing the necessity of an apology. Finally, she mumbled, "Sorry, Hannah. Didn't mean to."

"That wasn't very heartfelt," Mary said. "It sounded like an apology made only to achieve a result—to not get in trouble and to go to market."

Polly glared at her sister. "I said I was sorry, didn't I? I'm not going to beg. I'm not perfect like you."

"It's fine," Hannah said. "The apology was fine." She was quite sure she now understood nothing about having a sister. What was going on between Polly and Mary seemed at the moment to have very little to do with her.

"Do you want to go back?" Mary asked Hannah. "You must be upset."

But Hannah decided she wouldn't act upset. "No," she said. "We came to pick berries, so I think we should pick some. They look delicious." She picked up her pail and walked to the nearest bush.

For a time the three girls were silent, busily filling their pails with the large, firm berries. Hannah forced herself to be calm, and soon her heart was no longer pounding. She had never picked berries before, and she found she liked the process. For every two or three she picked, she stopped to taste one. They were tart and sweet at the same time, and their dark blue juice covered her hands.

When her pail was filled to the brim, Hannah sat down in the tall grass to rest. She pulled her knees up and rested her head on them, shading her eyes from the sun that had just emerged from behind billowing clouds.

With her eyes open but her head down, Hannah had a clear view of her pailful of berries. It was several feet away, directly in front of her. She was proud of her full pail, and looked forward to presenting it to Aunt Jane to make into tarts.

But suddenly, a pair of boots approached. She watched in horror as one boot shot forward and kicked the pail over, spilling all the berries. Hannah snapped her head up to see Polly standing in front of her.

"So sorry!" Polly said quickly. "That was an accident. I'm so clumsy!"

Hannah stood up and brushed off the skirt of her dress. She stared squarely at her cousin. "You did that on purpose. I saw you."

"You're always accusing me," Polly snapped. "It was an accident."

A million responses popped into Hannah's mind, but she was so angry she couldn't even speak. She'd had enough! This was it! She turned on her heel and walked away, heading straight for Gwenny. Mindlessly, she untied her horse and mounted with relative ease.

"Go!" she said, giving the reins a shake. "Let's get out of here, Gwenny!" In her anger and confusion, she reacted with pure instinct and rode as though she were completely used to it.

All the way back to the farm, horse and rider were a tightly working pair, each responding to the other.

"If only this ride could go on forever!" Hannah whispered to Gwenny, feeling proud and triumphant.

Market Day

Hannah stood just outside the open doorway that led to the kitchen and adjusted her bonnet. From her viewpoint she saw Aunt Jane hand Mary a small purse bulging with coins.

"Don't forget to buy tea," said Aunt Jane.

"And flour and sugar," said Mary, nodding. "I won't forget."

"Can we buy a sweet?" asked Polly.

"If there's any coin left over," said Aunt Jane, tugging at Polly's untied bonnet string. "And tie your bonnet, dear girl, so the wind doesn't send it flying."

Then Aunt Jane hurried outside to see if Ethan had the horses hitched to the wagon.

"I love market day!" Polly exclaimed, twirling around the kitchen in her best green dress. "It's my favorite day of the whole week."

"You're lucky you're going," Mary whispered to her sister, giving her a knowing look. "You're lucky that Hannah didn't tell on you about scaring Gwenny and kicking over her berries."

"It was an accident!" Polly hissed.

"Both times?" asked Mary.

"Yes, both times."

As Hannah started to enter the room, she heard Polly say, "And where is Hannah, anyway?"

"Changing her dress, I imagine," Mary answered.

"Mother let her have the first bath last night," Polly complained.

Hannah stalled at the doorway. She hated the thought of going in to face another scene.

"She's our guest," said Mary. "If we went to visit her, *we'd* get the first bath."

"But we'll never get to go to America!" Polly cried. "We're stuck here on this muddy farm! Hannah is the luckiest girl in the whole world!"

Hannah, not able to bear any more of Polly's complaining, hurried into the kitchen. Both girls turned to look at her.

"That's the most beautiful dress I've ever seen,"

Mary said. "May I feel the material?"

"Of course," Hannah said with a smile. It was the lavender silk that she had almost worn on her birthday back in Boston. The fabric was so pale it almost shimmered with silver, like the colors of early dawn. It hung from Hannah's waist in perfect, soft folds that swirled gracefully as she moved.

"My father brought back the silk from China and had the dress made for me in Boston," she told her cousins.

"It feels wonderful," Mary said. "You'll be the prettiest girl at market."

"I think that it's a bit fancy for market day," Polly sniffed. "Everyone will stare at her."

"She's wearing her best dress," Mary said evenly. "Just like we are."

"Yes," Polly admitted, "but our best dresses look like rags compared to hers. She's the queen and we're chamber maids."

"I'm sorry," Hannah said. Her face flushed with embarrassment. "I never meant to make you feel that way. I'll go change."

"No, you won't," said Mary. "You look perfectly wonderful. And we don't have time, anyway. If we don't leave right now we'll miss all the best goods."

Hannah tried to meet Polly's eyes, but Polly tossed

her head and hurriedly left the kitchen.

"Don't worry," said Mary. "Once we leave the farm, she'll perk up."

Outside, Uncle Ethan had hitched both Gwenny and another horse to a weathered wooden wagon. He finished straightening the double reins and handed them to Polly, who sat on the driver's seat.

The sight of Gwenny made Hannah feel better. She walked over and petted her affectionately. "How are you, Gwenny? Are you taking us to market?" Gwenny snorted an eager response and tossed her head.

"You've been taking good care of her," said Uncle Ethan to Hannah. "Her coat has never looked better."

"I love to brush her," Hannah said with a smile.

"And Mary tells me you're becoming a fine rider," he continued.

"Mary's a good teacher," Hannah replied. "And Gwenny is the best horse in the world!"

"That she is," Uncle Ethan agreed. "She'll fetch a good price at the horse auction in London this year."

"You're going to sell her?" Hannah asked, her smile fading with disbelief.

Uncle Ethan laughed and patted Gwenny on the flank. "We sell all but a few horses each year, Hannah. That's what one does on a horse farm."

"Who will buy her?" asked Hannah, not wanting to believe that Gwenny wouldn't stay on the farm forever and be lovingly tended by Mary or Uncle Ethan. She couldn't bear to think of Gwenny going to perfect strangers.

"Oh, a carriage company, no doubt. Hackneys make the best carriage horses around."

"That's how we get our money," Polly said. "But you wouldn't know about that."

"Polly! That was rude!" her father said sternly. "Apologize and in future hold your tongue about such matters."

"I'm sorry," Polly said quickly.

Hannah sensed that she did not want to jeopardize her opportunity to go to market.

"All right then," said Uncle Ethan. "You'd best be going. Have a nice time. And hold on to that purse, Mary."

Polly snapped the reins and the horses took off, turning right on the main road to town. Hannah watched Polly, admiring how well she drove the horses. She had such confidence. Nothing seemed to frighten her.

"You're so good at driving the wagon," Hannah told her from the back seat. "They don't let girls do that in Boston."

"I've been doing it since I was seven," Polly said. "You just have to let the horses know who's in charge."

"With Polly, you always know who's in charge," Mary joked, giving her sister a gentle shove on the arm.

"Well," Polly said with a laugh, "someone has to be in charge around here."

Polly had a wonderful, rich laugh. Hannah realized that she'd rarely heard it. Around Hannah, Polly was somber and spiteful. She wished she could make Polly laugh the way Mary had just done.

The horses were moving fast now, taking high steps with their strong legs. The wind blew in the girls' faces as the wagon bumped over the muddy road. It wasn't as much fun as riding Gwenny, but Hannah still enjoyed the ride.

Then suddenly a gust of wind hit them from the side, and Polly's untied bonnet blew right off her head.

"Oh, no!" Polly cried. "My best bonnet!"

"You didn't remember to tie it," Mary said. "Mother warned you."

Polly stopped the wagon and got out. Her bonnet, floating in the middle of a puddle, was soaked with mud. She held it out in front of her by a thumb and forefinger, staring in disgust.

"Look at this! I can't wear it! And now my hair is a mess. I'll be the worst-looking girl in town today!"

"You look lovely," Hannah offered. In the sunlight Polly's hair shone with golden highlights. "You have pretty hair."

Polly turned on Hannah, with spite in her eyes. "You can afford to say that, can't you? You know full well that *you're* the prettiest girl, with your silk dresses and silk bonnets!"

Hannah sat silently, hoping that Polly's anger would wear itself out. It seemed, however, just to have gotten started.

"Why, you're the luckiest girl in the whole world," Polly continued. "Your father is a sea captain and you've traveled around the world! You live in America; you're rich; you own hundreds of dresses; and you eat sweets every day! Mary and I are not so lucky. Or haven't you noticed? We're stuck on the farm. The only place we go is to market once a week."

When Polly was through, Hannah glanced at Mary, but even she didn't seem to know what to say. Hannah thought for a moment about all that Polly had revealed.

"Some of what you say is true," Hannah finally said. "But *you* are lucky, too."

71

"How am *I* lucky?" Polly said.

"Well, you have a wonderful, loving mother who's alive and well. She cares about you, worries about you. I'd give away every pretty dress and more for that. And you have a father who's home each and every day, not away on long voyages for months upon months. And you have a sister to confide in. And you have beautiful, elegant horses to ride whenever you want. Yes, Polly, I think you're lucky. Why don't you?"

Polly swallowed and stared at Hannah. "I never dreamed that you would think *we're* lucky," she said.

"I do," Hannah repeated. "I truly do."

Polly seemed about to say something, but then apparently changed her mind. She snapped the reins, and once again they were off.

Cousins at Last

When they reached town, Polly jumped down from her perch and expertly tied the wagon and horses to a hitching post. Then she took off running.

"Polly!" cried Mary. "Come back! Don't you want money for a sweet?"

But Polly was gone, disappearing into the large crowd of buyers and sellers.

"Where did she go?" Hannah asked.

"She always goes off to meet friends," said Mary. "Polly loves to gossip."

"Town life does seem to suit her," Hannah agreed. "She would certainly appreciate all the amusements and diversions a big city has to offer. Then she could always be right in the thick of things."

Hannah followed Mary into the crowd, taking in the colorful sights, sounds, and smells: freshly baked rolls, roasted meat, sharp cheeses, and apple cider. A rich variety of odors wafted through the air, making her mouth water. Vendors called from makeshift tables, exclaiming the worth of their candles, cloth, tools, medicines, and sweets, while their customers, picking the goods to examine, tried to get a better price. The mood was festive as the townspeople bought their necessities and then splurged on special treats to be had only on market day.

As Mary picked her way through the crowd and selected her items, Hannah had to work hard not to bump into women carrying overstuffed baskets and men with children perched on their shoulders. She listened to the conversations around her, enjoying the way the people sounded with their distinct accents.

As Mary selected a tin of tea and handed several coins to a stooped old gentleman, Hannah suddenly noticed a woman selling bonnets and shoes from behind a stall heaped with white, red, and yellow potatoes.

"Excuse me," she said to Mary. "I'll be right back."

"Hello," said the woman, seeing Hannah approach. "May I help you?"

"Yes," said Hannah. "I would like to buy two of your very finest bonnets. Silk, if you have them."

The woman stared at Hannah. "I have silk, miss, but it will cost you a pretty penny."

"Cost is not a consideration. They are gifts for my cousins. How about that green one over there? And the pink one?"

The woman placed the bonnets carefully in two hat boxes and took Hannah's money. Hannah was glad her father had remembered to give her English money when they'd arrived in London.

"What do you have there?" Mary asked, spotting Hannah and her two boxes.

"You'll see," Hannah replied, mysteriously. "But not until we meet up with Polly."

"No doubt she's at the wagon," Mary said, looking around. "She usually meets me there."

And, indeed, Polly was pacing impatiently by the wagon, pushing her blonde hair away from her face. "There you are!" she called. "I thought you were never coming."

"I stopped to buy you a sweet," Mary said, handing her sister a peppermint stick. "And one for Hannah and me, too."

"I also have something for you," Hannah said to Polly. "But first you must close your eyes."

"Whatever for?" Polly asked.

"Come now. It's something very nice, I promise."

"But no one would blame you a bit, if you put a snake in her hand," Mary said with a laugh.

Hannah laughed with her cousin, then insisted again that Polly close her eyes. Finally, Polly agreed. When her eyes were tightly shut, Hannah opened the first box and placed the green bonnet in Polly's hands.

"Now open!" she said.

Polly opened her eyes and gasped. "It's beautiful!" she said. "Is it really for me?"

"Yes!" Hannah said. "It's yours to keep. Just be sure to always tie it tight so that it doesn't end up in a mud puddle."

To Hannah's surprise, Polly's eyes brimmed with tears. She ran to Hannah and pulled her into an embrace. "Thank you," she whispered. "It's the nicest gift I've ever received. And I surely don't deserve it, I know. I've been awful to you."

Hannah hugged her back. "I'm glad you like it." Then she turned to face Mary. "I haven't forgotten

you," she said. She reached into the second box for the pale pink bonnet. "I thought the color would go well with your complexion."

Mary, too, was touched by her cousin's generosity. "Mother won't believe her eyes. We'll look like ladies."

"I can't wait to see it in Mother's dressing mirror," Polly said, twirling around. "It matches my dress so beautifully!"

"You both look wonderful," Hannah said with a sigh. "I can't believe I'm saying this, but I'm going to miss you when I leave—*both* of you. And Gwenny, of course."

Hannah went over and put her arms around Gwenny's neck. Gwenny eyed her seriously, as though she too understood that Hannah's visit was coming to an end.

"You know something?" Polly said. Her eyes were filled with surprise. "I'm going to miss you, too. Truly. Having you here is the most exciting thing that ever happened to us. Why did I ruin it? I'm awful!"

"No, you're not," Hannah said soothingly. "You've made me realize how much I have and how nice it is to share."

"That's what cousins are for," said Mary, linking arms with Polly and Hannah.

CHAPTER
NINE

Leaving for Home

"**D**o you want to pick berries one last time?" Polly asked Hannah and Mary. "I promise I won't kick any berry pails or cause any trouble."

Hannah shrugged her shoulders, not feeling like doing much of anything. Today was the day her father was coming for her. In two days they would leave on *Cloud Song* for America. She was eager to see her father, but the thought of leaving Gwenny and her cousins made her feel sad and empty.

"It may be your last chance to ride Gwenny," Mary said quietly. "And it's a lovely day."

"I hate those words 'last chance,'" Hannah said with a sigh. "How will I ever say goodbye to Gwenny?"

"It'll be hard," Mary agreed. "We have to do it every year when our horses go to auction. You get very attached to them."

"They're just horses," Polly said. "It's harder for me to say goodbye to people. I'm going to miss you, Hannah, but at least I know I'll see you again."

"How," asked Mary, "do you suppose you'll see Hannah again?"

"I've got a plan," explained Polly. "When I'm a bit older, I'm going to sail to America and live there. I'm going to start saving my money by not buying sweets at market."

Mary and Hannah laughed at this, unable to imagine sweet-toothed Polly forgoing her weekly indulgence.

"This I will have to see to believe," said Mary.

"Watch me, then," said Polly good naturedly, making a funny face at her sister.

The change Polly had undergone in the final days of Hannah's visit was amazing. No more pranks or unkind comments or silent disdain. The three girls had finally been able to have the kind of fun Hannah had dreamed about. They rode together, worked in the stables, and sat by the fire in the evening telling stories. Each night Hannah entertained her cousins with another story of her travels around the world on

Cloud Song with her father.

"Berry picking, then?" Polly asked again. "We can't just sit here feeling sorry for ourselves."

"That's true enough," answered Hannah, standing up. "Let's go."

"I'll get the pails," Polly said.

"Hannah and I will get the horses," Mary said.

Inside the stables Gwenny was busy munching hay. She tossed her head when she spotted Hannah, and several pieces of hay fell from her mouth. Hannah reached forward to stroke the mare's soft ears. Gwenny was such a healthy horse. She never missed a meal and loved to be exercised and ridden.

"One more ride?" Hannah whispered to Gwenny. "When you're finished eating, of course!"

Gwenny nickered and stamped and finished a few more mouthfuls of breakfast. As Hannah watched her, she tried to memorize the outline of Gwenny's handsome form, and the specific shade of her chestnut brown color. If she closed her eyes, she could picture Gwenny's face exactly.

When the three girls had saddled their horses, they set out for the blueberry bushes. This time Hannah felt much more secure riding Gwenny. She handled the reins with comfort, and Gwenny easily responded to Hannah's gentle commands.

How strange it will feel, thought Hannah, when I go back to riding sidesaddle in Boston, after having ridden astride for these past weeks. If I get to ride, she reminded herself. Besides an occasional riding excursion at her friend Sarah's country house, Hannah doubted that she'd have much opportunity to ride once she was back home.

"I'm going to miss you," Hannah whispered to Gwenny, urging her into a quick canter. "Let's go fast! Let's fly with the wind."

At the berry bushes the girls filled their pails to the brim. But they also ate handfuls of the succulent fruit, not caring that the juice ran down their arms, staining their white aprons a dark blue. It didn't bother Hannah in the least, who had grown rather used to the casual country lifestyle, where no one cared if your apron was stained or your hair was not quite combed to perfection.

"Umm, these are delicious!" Polly declared. "And so sweet. Maybe I could eat these instead of toffee."

"Are you feeling quite well?" Mary teased. "You seem a bit off, lately."

"Maybe I am," Polly said with a laugh. "It's just such a relief not to have to hate Hannah any longer."

"A relief to me, too," Hannah said. "I think I had quite a large enough dose."

Polly, serious now, looked intently at her cousin. "Truthfully, Hannah, do you forgive me? I never *hated* you at all. I just was so—"

"So *envious*," Mary concluded. "Say it, Polly."

"It's true. I was envious of all I thought you had. But you showed me that we both have lots and lots."

"Well," said Hannah, "you've shown me things, too."

"Like what?" asked Mary.

"For one thing, I've learned that I put too much emphasis on how things look on the outside. You must have thought I was awful the way I reacted when you told me I had to help clean up after the horses."

Mary laughed, and Polly performed an impromptu demonstration of Hannah stepping gingerly over horse manure, imitating her wrinkled nose and look of revulsion.

"But now," said Hannah, "I'm a changed person." And with that, she took a fat berry from her pail and threw it directly at Polly's apron. "I've owed you that," she laughed.

Polly reached into her own pail and threw several back, hitting Hannah on the neck. Laughing, Hannah pelted berries at both Mary and Polly, dodging the ones that came flying back at her.

Breathless from laughter, the girls finally called an

end to the war. Each of them was covered with berry juice polka dots.

"That was fun!" Hannah cried. "I've never thrown a berry at anyone in my life." This was how she imagined a life shared with sisters might be.

"Do horses like berries?" Hannah asked, sitting up and wiping her hands.

"Probably," said Mary. "But don't give her too many. It might give her a stomachache."

Hannah went over and fed a handful to Gwenny, who nuzzled Hannah's hand looking for more.

"She liked them!" Hannah said. "All right, then, just a few more."

"Horses will eat anything," Polly said. "They'd eat an old paint bucket if you left it in their stall."

"Your love of horses is deeply touching," Hannah

replied. "I suppose you're going to become an animal doctor one day."

"Not on your life!" Polly cried. "I'm going to become an actress and travel the world."

"And Mary will be a great novelist," said Hannah.

"And what about you?" Polly asked. "What will you do? Become the first-ever female sea captain?"

"No," said Hannah. "I love the sea. But maybe *I'll* become an animal doctor." Though she spoke spontaneously, the idea held great appeal for Hannah. To be around animals, and to care for them and heal them, would be wonderful.

Later, alone in the stable, Hannah tried to say a private goodbye to Gwenny. But the words wouldn't come. So she did what she knew the horse loved best and brushed her over and over. Tears slid down Hannah's cheeks, and her throat felt raw from holding in so much emotion.

How strange, she thought, that now I love the smell of the stable. And all the chores that used to seem so difficult and tedious now just seem a part of daily life. In Hannah's mind, the rewards of being around horses far outweighed the responsibilities.

Just then the stable door creaked open. Hannah turned around, expecting Mary or Polly. But there stood her father, with his white beard and sparkling eyes.

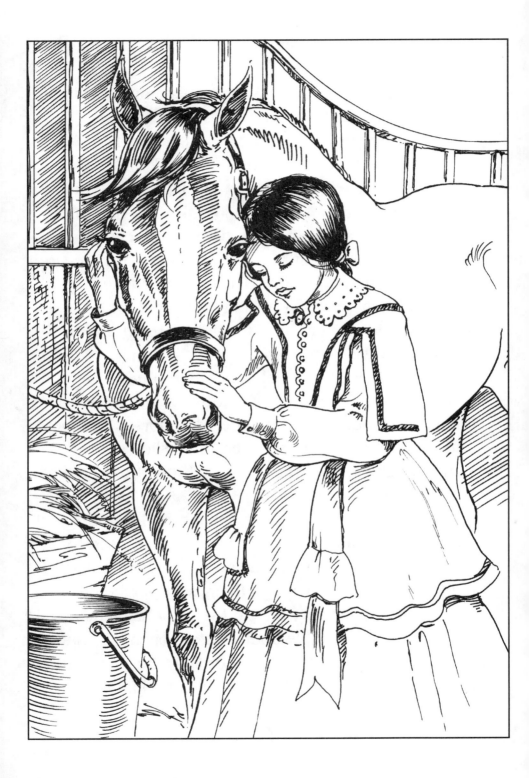

"Father!" she cried. "You're here!"

"I was told I'd find you here. Ethan says you practically live in the stable."

Hannah hugged her father tight, smelling the familiar scent of his pipe tobacco. He kissed her cheek and then held her at arm's length.

"You look different," he said.

"I do? How?"

"Let me see . . . older, maybe."

"Messier?"

"Perhaps."

"Life on the farm!" she said with a laugh. "I love it here. You're expected to look a mess sometimes."

"I think you look wonderful," he said. "Was your visit successful?"

"Yes!" Hannah answered. "Wonderful, and hard, and strange sometimes. Here, I want you to meet my horse, Gwenny. Well, not my horse, really, but a horse I've come to love . . . "

"So this is Gwenny," Captain Brooks said, holding out his hand for the horse to smell. "I was just talking to Ethan about her."

"You were? Why?"

"Well," said Captain Brooks, "it seems you won't have to say goodbye to her—yet."

"I won't?" For a second Hannah dared to hope

that she might get to keep Gwenny. That hope was quickly dashed.

"I'm going to take four of Ethan's best horses back to Boston and sell them for him—including Gwenny," explained her father.

"You're going to sell Gwenny?"

"Now, Hannah, you know we can't keep a horse. It's not practical."

"Why are you bringing them such a long way, only to sell them?"

"I can get Ethan a much better price back in the States. There's a big demand for purebred horses born and raised in England."

"Oh," Hannah whispered.

Her initial joy turned to heartache at the thought of selling Gwenny to a stranger in America who only cared about a horse's English breeding.

"But this way," her father said, "you can have her with you for the twelve-day journey to America. And though I've signed on a groom, he'll need your help, I'm sure. You've become quite an expert, Ethan tells me."

"Gwenny belongs on a farm! She shouldn't have to stay in a livery in the middle of Boston!" Hannah exclaimed, and she ran past her father and out the stable.

The next day it was time to say goodbye for real.

As a driver loaded Hannah's trunk onto the carriage, the three cousins stood in silence, heads bent.

Captain Brooks strode up to the sad-looking group. "I have an announcement to make," he said, in his best sea captain manner.

Hannah wondered what it would be. He was certainly full of strange plans.

"Polly and Mary," he began, "I have an offer to make to you. I've already received permission from your parents. So, if it's agreeable to you both, here's the plan. Next year Hannah and I will sail to England again and bring you back with us. You can spend the summer with us in Boston, where we can return your hospitality."

Polly and Mary jumped up and down with delight and hugged one another. Hannah joined in, as surprised by the news as her cousins were.

"Oh, Father," Hannah said excitedly, "do you mean it? Really?"

"Really and truly," he replied. "It's nice to see your smile again, Hannah. I thought it had disappeared forever."

"Then we don't really have to say goodbye," Mary said, sniffing into her handkerchief.

"Now don't you start crying, Mary," Polly scolded, "or I'll start crying, too."

"And then I'll join in," said Hannah.

"And then we'll have to go inside and get our umbrellas to stay dry," Ethan said. "And today the sun is shining."

Hannah hugged Ethan, kissing him lightly on the cheek. Then she nestled into Jane's full, motherly embrace, smelling the just-baked bread on her aunt's white apron.

"Thank you for everything," she said. "I'll never forget my time here."

Then the three girls said goodbye, breaking their agreement not to cry.

"See you in a year," Hannah told her almost-sisters. "Write me a letter soon."

"We will," they promised. "See you in a year!"

"The horses will be at the docks tomorrow?" Captain Brooks asked Ethan.

"Bright and early," Ethan said. "I've got it all arranged."

"Well, then, we're off," Captain Brooks said. He took his daughter's hand and helped her step reluctantly into the carriage.

Inside, Hannah turned and waved to Mary and Polly until they became tiny dots on the road behind her.

See you tomorrow, Gwenny! thought Hannah. At least I have that to look forward to.

Horses On Board

"Hello, Gwenny!" Hannah stood on the ship's deck, watching as the horse groom led Gwenny up the ramp leading to *Cloud Song*. Gwenny probably couldn't hear her over the din of working sailors, Hannah decided. But she called again, anyway.

Gwenny seemed to be resisting the groom. Every few steps forward, she stopped and looked back, as if sensing she was leaving behind the land of her birth. Hannah wanted to go to her and calm her. But she had promised her father that she would stay out of the way until the horses were settled in their stalls below.

Gwenny was the last horse to be loaded, so

Hannah knew she could visit the animals within the hour. She couldn't wait to see Gwenny, to stroke her and to calm her. It would be so strange for Gwenny to be taken suddenly from the farm and put inside the bottom of a ship for twelve days. Hannah hated to think about it.

"What's the matter?" said Captain Brooks, meeting up with his daughter on the deck. "Where's that smile?"

"Oh, Father!" said Hannah. "I'm so worried about Gwenny and the other horses. It will be so strange for them."

"True," her father agreed. "But I've transported many animals over the years, and they've always arrived safely. Gwenny will be fine."

"I hope so," Hannah said. "I already feel as though I've betrayed her trust."

"Not at all," said Captain Brooks. "She'll have you with her, and I've hired the best groom available. Have you met him yet?"

"No," said Hannah. "But I watched him bringing Gwenny up the ramp. What is his name?"

"Mr. Steele. Oliver Steele. A good fellow."

"May I go below now and meet him?" Hannah asked.

"Only if you promise me that you'll let Mr. Steele

do his job, and you won't interfere."

"I promise," Hannah said solemnly. "I just want to see Gwenny and make sure she's all right."

In the darkness of the cargo hold, Hannah located the temporary horse stalls. She could see Mr. Steele tying a brown mare named Cecily to her stall. The horses were whinnying to each other, trying to make sense of their surroundings.

"Do you need any help?" Hannah asked as she approached. "I'm Hannah Brooks."

"The captain's daughter, eh?" Mr. Steele asked. He was tall and thin, perhaps in his late forties. He had curly gray hair and a crisp gray moustache. The most distinguishing characteristic of all, though, was the black patch he wore over his left eye. "I heard you have a real love of horses."

"That's true," Hannah answered. "Gwenny, the chestnut mare over there, is the horse I'm fondest of."

"Ah, Gwenny, is it? I haven't got all their names, yet. She's a pretty one, to be sure."

Just then, Gwenny whinnied, and the others joined in.

"Are the horses all right?" Hannah asked.

"Just getting used to things," Mr. Steele explained. "Once I give them food and water, they'll quiet down."

"Have you always worked with horses?" Hannah

asked, curious about this gentle man with the strange eye patch.

"Just about my whole life," he answered. "My father was a groom, so it's in my blood I suppose. Can't stay away from the creatures—even when an injured stallion kicked me hard and put my eye out."

Hannah gasped. She had never witnessed a violent horse, and she couldn't imagine Gwenny hurting anyone. "How awful for you," Hannah said.

"Oh, that's all right, miss. I'm used to it by now. And the horse couldn't help himself. He took a bad tumble off a slippery hill."

From her stall Gwenny whinnied again.

"May I try to calm Gwenny?" Hannah asked.

Mr. Steele nodded his permission. "They're all tied now. I'm going to fill these water buckets from that barrel over there."

Hannah moved to the front end of the stall, calling softly to Gwenny. The horse stopped and was silent, turning her head to follow Hannah's voice.

"How are you, pretty girl?" Hannah asked, reaching to unlatch the stall door. She entered and stood by Gwenny's side, patting her flank. "Everything is fine, Gwenny. I'm with you now, and I'll be here the entire journey."

Gwenny nickered and tossed her head. Hannah

reached into her pocket and brought out a small clump of radishes. "These are for you. Cook gave them to me for you."

Gwenny sniffed at the radishes but didn't eat them. "Are you too excited to eat?" Hannah asked. "That happens to me, when I travel." She put the radishes back in her pocket.

It made Hannah both happy and sad to be with her horse. The happy part was simply being in the horse's presence, smelling her earthy scent and touching her soft mane. But the sad part was knowing that she couldn't ride Gwenny or exercise her. All she could do was talk to her, brush her coat, and bring her special treats from the ship's galley.

Hannah also missed her cousins. She wished they

were with her right then. The three girls could laugh and talk and explore the ship together. And Mary knew all four of the horses so well, which might make their voyage easier.

I'm back to being an only child, Hannah thought. And when I get back to Boston, it will be just Fiona and me in our big quiet house.

Gwenny took a small step to nuzzle Hannah's shoulder. "You always cheer me up," she told the horse, rubbing Gwenny's soft neck. "That's one thing we can do for each other these next twelve days."

Late that night, after *Cloud Song* had been under sail for many hours, Hannah woke up in her stateroom with a start. She had a funny feeling, and she couldn't figure out quite where it came from. Maybe she was a touch seasick, though that rarely happened to her. Maybe something from the lavish dinner had upset her stomach. Or maybe it was Gwenny!

Remembering the horses, Hannah got up from her small bunk and pulled on her white silk dressing gown and Chinese slippers. She tiptoed out of her quarters, closing the door softly behind her. Hoping she wouldn't run into her father, she went below to check on the horses.

It was dark in the cargo hold, except for the light

of a single oil lantern that Mr. Steele had left hanging on its special hook.

Instantly, Hannah knew something was wrong.

A terrible thumping noise came from one of the stalls, a banging that made the boards shake. And one of the horses was moaning, making a low, eerie sound.

When she got closer, Hannah discovered that the moans came from Gwenny.

"What's the matter?" she asked, trying to keep panic from her voice. "Are you sick, Gwenny?"

Gwenny threw herself against the wall, groaning with pain. Then she jerked around and kicked at her belly with her hind legs. It seemed to Hannah that the horse was trying to turn her muzzle to look at her side.

"Is it your stomach?" Hannah asked, her heart pounding.

Hannah noticed that Gwenny's water pail was still full and that she hadn't eaten any of her feed. Hannah remembered the radishes Gwenny had refused earlier.

A dozen thoughts raced through her head. Could Gwenny be seasick? But the other horses seemed fine, if fairly alarmed by Gwenny's behavior. They paced in their stalls, calling to each other.

Then Hannah had another horrible thought.

Perhaps it was the berries she had fed Gwenny yesterday on the farm. Mary had warned her that they could give the horse a stomachache. Had Hannah inadvertently made her own horse this sick?

"Oh, Gwenny!" Hannah called. "I'm so sorry! Please forgive me, Gwenny."

She tried to reach inside the stall, but Gwenny slammed against the door, almost pinning Hannah's hand. Suddenly Hannah remembered Mr. Steele's experience of being kicked by a horse. But Gwenny wouldn't hurt her, would she?

Gwenny's frantic movements were becoming more intense. Hannah had to do something, before the horse hurt herself.

"I'll be right back!" Hannah cried. "I have to get Mr. Steele! He'll know what to do!"

For an answer, Gwenny threw herself against the stall once again.

The noise thundered in Hannah's ears as she ran to the stairs.

The Long Night

Mr. Steele watched as Gwenny thrashed against the sides of her stall, still moaning in pain. The other horses, frightened by Gwenny's wild behavior, whinnied back and forth. The sounds echoed throughout the bottom of the ship and seemed almost deafening.

"What's wrong with her?" Hannah asked, unable to keep from trembling. She hadn't remembered to bring a blanket or shawl.

"From the looks of her," Mr. Steele said, "from the way she's kicking at her sides, she probably has colic."

"Colic?" asked Hannah.

"Basically, it's a very bad stomachache," said Mr. Steele.

"Could it be from eating berries? I fed her some yesterday."

"No, Hannah, you didn't cause this," he answered. He seemed to sense the guilt she was feeling. "Horses get colic from stress and being overexcited—such as being taken from familiar surroundings and being put on a ship."

"Can you do *something* for Gwenny?" Hannah asked.

Mr. Steele's face grew sober as he watched Gwenny. "I've had my share of experience with colicky horses," he answered, "and I won't lie to you, Hannah. It's a very grave situation. The next few hours are crucial."

Tears sprang instantly to Hannah's eyes. "What can we do? We have to try something!"

"We will. Right now I am going to my room to get some equipment. Then I will wake your father. He must be consulted in this matter."

"Yes," said Hannah, eager for her father's calm presence.

"And Hannah," Mr. Steele continued, "you must promise not to go near Gwenny. At the moment she's extremely dangerous."

Hannah looked at Mr. Steele's eye patch and nodded.

After he had gone, Hannah paced outside Gwenny's stall. She didn't know what else to do. She couldn't touch her, and she couldn't think of a way to quiet the other animals. She felt absolutely helpless.

"Please hurry back," she said to herself. "Please help Gwenny. I can't lose her. She has to get better!"

Finally, Mr. Steele and Captain Brooks returned. Hannah ran to her father and cried against his shoulder. He held her tight, but all the while he watched as Gwenny thrashed in her stall.

"I'm sorry, Hannah," her father told her. "This must be difficult for you."

"Can we do *something*?" Hannah pleaded.

"Mr. Steele has a few remedies to try. But Hannah, I must warn you. If she doesn't get better, we'll have no choice but to put Gwenny out of her misery."

"You mean shoot her?" gasped Hannah. "No, Father! No!"

"Sometimes it's the more humane thing to do," Mr. Steele said quietly. "It's cruel to leave an animal to suffer when there's no hope of a recovery."

"But we can't give up hope!" Hannah cried. "Not yet!"

"Hannah, try to stay calm," said her father, "for

Gwenny's sake. We'll do everything possible, but as captain of this ship, I can't allow a horse to suffer needlessly."

Hannah nodded through her tears and watched as Mr. Steele began mixing a strange concoction in what looked like old wine bottles.

"What's that?" she asked, her voice quavering.

"It's called a drench bottle," Mr. Steele said. "It's the only way we'll be able to get any medicine down her throat. She won't take it voluntarily, believe me."

"What's the medicine?" Hannah asked.

"A mixture of ether and laudanum in plain old water. That's what my book on horse diseases recommends. But there are no guarantees, even with medicine."

When he had finished, Mr. Steele stood up and looked at Captain Brooks. "Can you help me hold the horse?" he asked. "Hannah, take this bottle and hand it to me when we've got hold of Gwenny."

Hannah took the bottle and watched as Mr. Steele opened the latch of the stall, talking quietly and moving slowly toward the sick horse. He managed to grab the lead, only to lose it when Gwenny jerked away. Mr. Steele tried again, and this time he was successful.

"Hannah, hand me the bottle," Mr. Steele said. His

voice was calm and businesslike, so as not to alert Gwenny to what was coming. "Captain, come to the left side."

But Gwenny wouldn't let Captain Brooks near her. She shied away from him again and again as he tried to steady her head for the medicine.

"I'm afraid I'm not going to be much help," Captain Brooks said, moving away. "I can't get near her."

"May I try?" asked Hannah, moving forward. "I think I might be able to calm her, at least until you give the medicine. She trusts me."

"No!" said Captain Brooks. "Absolutely not. I forbid it."

"He's right," agreed Mr. Steele, still struggling to keep his hold on the horse.

"Just for a few seconds?" Hannah persisted. "I'll move away if it doesn't work. Please Father? I'll never be able to forgive myself if something happens to Gwenny, and I didn't at least try to help."

Captain Brooks looked at his daughter's distraught and tear-stained face. Then he looked to Mr. Steele, as if for guidance. Mr. Steel shrugged, and the two men seemed to silently agree to let Hannah have her chance.

"Move slowly," coached Mr. Steele. "Start talking to her so she hears your voice. Touch her the way that you always have. Where does she liked to be stroked?"

"On her ears and neck," Hannah said, moving slowly forward. "Hey, Gwenny, it's me—Hannah. Hey, girl, how are you? Don't worry, Gwenny, everyone gets sick the first time they're on board a ship."

Hannah wasn't sure that Gwenny heard anything over the din of the horses. But finally she was by Gwenny's side, close enough to reach out and touch her neck.

"Shhh, Gwenny, it's all right," Hannah soothed, reaching to stroke the horse.

"Keep talking," said Mr. Steele. "I think she's responding to your voice."

Hannah kept talking and stroking Gwenny's neck. After a time the animal quieted and stopped thrashing long enough for Mr. Steele to raise her head high and tip the bottle down her throat.

Gwenny obviously didn't care for the taste and sputtered a good deal of it at Mr. Steele as she backed away from him.

"Be careful!" said Captain Brooks, never taking his eyes off his daughter.

"There you go," Hannah calmly said to Gwenny. "Good girl. That's going to help you feel better."

"Did you get any in?" Captain Brooks asked.

"Some," Mr. Steele answered. "But we have to

repeat the dosage two more times at ten-minute intervals."

"Hannah, why don't you go back to bed and get some rest? You look exhausted," her father advised.

"No," Hannah said. "I'm not the least bit tired. Besides, Gwenny likes having me here. See? I help her stay calm. And she still has to have two more doses of medicine."

Captain Brooks tugged at his beard, studying his daughter and the horse at her side. "I might not understand your attachment to this animal, Hannah, my dear," he said at last, "but I can't help but be impressed by the courage you've shown tonight." Then he turned to Mr. Steele. "I need to go above and check on the night watch. Do you want me to send down a sailor or two to help?"

"I'll alert you if we need extra hands," Mr. Steele said. "Just hand me that second drench bottle."

"I'll return shortly," said Captain Brooks, passing the medicine bottle. "Hannah, you must listen to Mr. Steele. Do you promise?"

"I promise," Hannah answered, not looking up. She didn't want to be distracted from her job of calming Gwenny.

And Gwenny *was* calmer, or so it seemed to Hannah.

"Is she better?" Hannah asked. "Is it working?"

"Only time will tell," Mr. Steele answered.

The second dose went down a little easier, with less of it spit back at Mr. Steele.

As Gwenny quieted, the other three horses quieted, too. Hannah felt her muscles straining with tension, and she stifled a yawn. She was exhausted, both physically and mentally, but she refused to give up until Gwenny was well again.

"I won't let you die," she whispered to Gwenny.

In the early dawn, long after Gwenny's third dose of medicine, Captain Brooks returned below to check once again on the situation. Mr. Steele, seated on a wooden crate, was fast asleep, his head resting on a barrel. Gwenny was also asleep, lying down on the straw in her stall. Hannah, however, was wide awake, leaning against the door to Gwenny's stall.

"How is she?" Captain Brooks asked, squatting down next to his daughter.

"Better," Hannah yawned, stretching. "Mr. Steele said we should bring her up on deck later and walk her around. The exercise will help ease the stress in her stomach. Will that be allowed?"

"I'll arrange it," he assured her. "You should go to bed."

"Just a little longer," Hannah said. "Until we're

sure Gwenny's really out of danger."

"I'm very impressed with how you reacted to this," said Captain Brooks. "You've helped save Gwenny's life. You're a very strong young lady."

"Yes," said Hannah, struggling to her feet. "I helped save my horse—only to have her sold to a complete stranger when we get back to Boston!"

A Boston Tea Party

"That must have been the longest night in your life!" Fiona exclaimed. She had just finished hearing Hannah's recounting of the night Gwenny was sick on *Cloud Song*.

"It was," Hannah agreed. "But at least Gwenny recovered."

"Then why are you lookin' so sad?" Fiona asked, reaching over to add more tea to Hannah's empty cup. The two of them were enjoying a cozy chat together, catching up on all the things that had happened during their long separation.

"I'm sad because today Gwenny and the other horses are being taken to a horse broker," explained

Hannah. "I'll never see her again. I know Uncle Ethan needs the money, but I still wish she was back on the farm."

"Of course you do," Fiona said. She refilled her own cup, then passed Hannah a plate of lemon cookies.

Hannah shook her head. "I'm not hungry," she said.

"Try to think about the brave thing you did in helpin' to save the poor creature," Fiona suggested. "She wouldn't be alive if not for you. That was an act of pure charity."

"I'm not feeling very charitable right now," Hannah said with a sigh. "Maybe I'll take a nap."

"Of course, darlin'," said Fiona. "You must be exhausted, and here I am tryin' to extract every last detail of your grand adventure. Let's get you upstairs."

Just then Captain Brooks came striding in, still

wearing his sailing clothes. "Hannah, come with me," he said in a very serious tone. "I have something to show you."

"What is it?" Hannah asked. She yawned, not wanting to move from her comfortable chair. "Must I?"

"Yes. Come see," he urged, taking Hannah's hand.

Captain Brooks led Hannah out of the room to the hall vestibule and opened the heavy front door. There in the street stood a chestnut Hackney horse that looked very much like Gwenny. Hannah thought she surely was seeing a mirage, for how could Gwenny be in front of her house when she had been delivered to a horse broker?

"Gwenny?" Hannah asked with confusion. Maybe she was so tired she wasn't thinking clearly.

But the second the horse snorted a greeting, Hannah knew it *was* Gwenny. She ran to the street and threw her arms around the beautiful chestnut horse.

"I thought she was sold!" Hannah cried.

"She was," answered her father.

"Oh," said Hannah, not understanding.

"To me!" her father announced.

"What?" Hannah and Fiona gasped in unison.

"After I saw how you cared for her on the journey, I knew the two of you belonged together. I couldn't be

the one to separate such a pair."

"Oh, Father!" Hannah cried. "Thank you, thank you! This is the happiest day of my life."

Captain Brooks hugged his daughter, smiling at her happiness. "I bought her for you so you won't feel lonely. We'll board her in the country, and you can ride her on weekends and vacations."

"Wait until I write this news to Polly and Mary," Hannah said. "They won't believe that Gwenny is staying in the family!"

Hannah gleefully stroked Gwenny's face, still not quite believing that the horse was hers.

"Welcome to America," Hannah told her beloved horse. "Welcome *home*!"

FACTS
ABOUT THE BREED

You probably know a lot about Hackneys from reading this book. Here are some more interesting facts about this high-stepping English breed.

Ω Hackney horses generally stand between 14 and 15.3 hands high. Instead of using feet and inches, all horses are measured in hands and inches. A hand is equal to four inches.

Ω Hackney ponies can be as small as 12.2 hands, but they cannot exceed 14 hands.

Ω Hackneys are usually bay (brown with a black mane and tail), brown, or chestnut (reddish-brown with the same color mane and tail).

∩ The Hackney has a slightly convex profile and a small head. The ears and the muzzle are also small, while the eyes are large.

∩ The legs are on the short side with strong hocks, which are low to the ground. The hooves are allowed to grow long to emphasize the horse's action.

∩ The Hackney has a compact body, strong shoulders, low withers, and a long neck, which it carries high. The tail also is elevated, particularly when the horse is in motion. Hackneys originated in England. They are descended from Norfolk and Yorkshire Roadsters, trotting horses that had become popular in the 1700s. These horse were crossed with Thoroughbreds, and the Hackney Horse was born.

∩ The Hackney Horse Society was founded in 1883 in England. The society publishes a stud book and works to improve and promote Hackney horses and ponies. They also hold an annual horse show in Sussex, England, during the month of June. In addition, the society maintains the Hackney Museum.

∩ The American Hackney Horse Society, which was founded in 1890 and has its headquarters in Lexington, Kentucky, also registers both Hackney horses and ponies.

∩ A pony named 239 Stella was the first Hackney pony to come to America. A. J. Cossatt, who was instrumental in founding the American Hackney Horse Society, brought her to Philadelphia in 1878.

∩ Early Hackneys were of two types, the heavier coach animal and the lighter horse. The larger animal was used by the British Army and was exported to improve military horses in Australia, Finland, France, Germany, Holland, Hungary, and Italy.

∩ The lighter Hackney, a horse ideally suited to pull an elegant carriage, is the type of Hackney seen today.

∩ Today, although some Hackneys are ridden as pleasure horses, most Hackneys are show horses. They compete in in-hand classes, where they are judged on how well they move and on conformation. Hackneys also compete in driving classes, such as the Concourse d'Elegance, Private Driving, and Carriage Driving Trials.

∩ The famous Hackney mare Nonpareil was said to have trotted 100 miles pulling a carriage in just under 9 hours and 57 minutes.

∩ Although Hackneys are known for their trotting ability and high action, they also make great jumpers. At the 1936 Berlin Olympics, a Hackney named Tosca won the gold for the German team. In 1910 another Hackney, Confidence, cleared 7 feet 2 inches at the National Horse Show in New York City. Later he went on to sail over a fence 8 feet 1.5 inches high. Sir Ashton, the winner of the New York National high jump in 1915, actually made it over an 8 foot 2 inch fence at a show in Chicago.

∩ Today Hackney horses and ponies are raised all over the world. The Netherlands probably breeds most of these stylish horses. The breed is also popular in Canada, England, South Africa, and the United States.